Dominus
Lacrimarum

By: A.T. Soto

Dominus Lacrimarum

By: A.T. Soto (Iudex Luciferian)

Those who showed me no mercy with unwarranted cruelty; know that I will be waiting. I will have such unimaginable sights to show you; and you can not escape.

PATER; IN ME CONSOLATOR TEMPUS DESPERATIONIS. OMNES ENIM HABEO, EST

NIHIL IN PLENA. REDDE MIHI LAETITIA PATRE, IN TEMPORE TRISTITAE. HOC

MIHI GAUDIUM PERDITA MUNDO.

ITA FIAT!

NEMA

Human evolution has failed to be attained due to
worldwide corruption, pollution, greed, exploitation
and stupidity (to name a few). As a result, most have
failed to be rehabilitated from their almost irreversible
state of frivolity, superficiality, apathy and willing
dehumanization via mundane, recreational
degeneracy. In a nutshell – we have failed to grasp the
meaning,
Behind the quality of life.
Only a select few CHOSEN souls in the eyes of the
Gods, or alien beings (whatever you choose to call
them); have been favored for preservation. This of
course, has NOTHING to do with social class, as the
elite would have you believe; for they are the main
source of that mass corruption, with the United States
being its stronghold.

The evidence of this, is everywhere! We have a
legalized, murder for profit health care system; a
nationwide, plutocratic breeding ground for
Universities - that also counteracts, as a catalyst for
mass mediocrity. One nation fueled by radical evil;
and a hyper, fear mongering media. A media that
nurtures and fosters the very worst aspects of human
nature,
in order to inscribe a mass illusion of success.
Religion of course, remains its biggest ally in this
insidious modus operandi, as a grotesque collaborator
of sorts, instilling mind control.

And no, I will not elucidate further about these beings
who created us, and have grown beyond tired; of
witnessing most of us turn repeatedly into nothing
more than genetic excrement. Their blessings, rewards
and kindness extend only to their beloved seed – The
Chosen (and the Chosen's associates). If you believe

this to be daft, absurd or heresy; know that you were created with very little value in mind to begin with.

Also be aware, it is not I who will be set on trial for reading these works – it is the reader. In a world that clearly thrives on distorted morals, sanctimony; and dishonor. I could give one bloody fuck about its impending accusations, and\or convictions. I have undoubtedly, but one thing to offer the garbage who aims to defame; and that's threefold the pain, that I unjustly endured within this lifetime thus far – compliments of The Dark Trinity (the main force behind this design). All literary pieces are a testimony of my raison d'etre, and were channeled precisely.

This book is meant to resonate, AGAIN – within a SELECT FEW. Blessed be those brilliant minds, deliberately banished by worldly mediocrity, and provincial frivolity. Here's to YOU! Monsters, mutants, and rejects of a globe fueled by systematic cruelty, cowardice, treachery and facile remedies. I reject recognition from all acolytes of such abhorrent guidelines for success. My true brothers and sisters of ALL SHUNNED PATHS, YOU ARE WHAT MATTERS TO ME.
For those rejected by this Earth, are most likely to have redeeming value after all.....enjoy these poems and stories.

- A.T. Soto (Iudex Luciferian)

For: Kimbal Summers (My greatest teacher)

" For in our world – the hybrid heart is evil, hence in constant conflict with its own malevolence; therefore it must be forced to discern such power, outside the limitations of their limited, to almost non existent divine qualities "

- Yours truly.

The Dark Prince

Come away O chosen soul;
To the crimson rivers as life unfolds,
With a satyr hand in hand.
For the world's more full of treachery;
Than you can understand.

Let my love guide you.....Protect you.
May the elements comfort you; as your realm is
weaved by the tears of The Fallen, and the heart of the
divine.

I bestow you my son;
The unknown kindness...
The forbidden knowledge...
The unseen mercy, the others will never know.

Let no hand touch you, or hinder
You under the flames of my care;
And may you rest in my embrace
From afar; until we meet again.

12/09/14

Obscurum, Amicus Meus

With sobbing, grief stricken knees I kneel before a
colossal tidal wave – frozen before me, as I hold a
bouquet of flowers.
This giant wave holds an ancient name. It is locked,
within the very core of my being.
Now I've come to you, as you came to me in a
childhood dream.
ALL I ASK...

Is that you tend to me dearly at your seaside; safe and
sound, and in higher ground.
I shall lead the guilty to this appointed place; holding
the crimson jar bearing the names of my assailants,
defamers and tormentors.

And by the sign of The Blood Harvest Moon, RISE once
more and guide my hand; as I hurl these names into
the dark might of your abysmal waters. Enki – Great
Elder! Let us witness from the Onyx colored boulders;
and assuage our thirst, for universal justice.

1/08/15

The Calling of The Onyx Chalice

Come forth, divine pariahs of tomorrow.

Let the stars shower you in alien mercy for time
indefinite; in frivolous nights filled with pain, and
strange upheaval.

Cry out to HIM, and he shall collect every tear unto his
onyx chalice – and with it; darkened rainbows under
shades of violet horizons, will foreshadow the coming
of a new reign.

A reign of undefiled truth and wisdom. Beneath the
heel, of those who suffer presently; bearing the sigil –
marking this glorious time.

Cry with me Nephilim...and be not proud.
Let his chalice overflow with the wrath of legends, by
joining me in this battle – sealing the seal, of all seals.

3/20/15

What Is Normal?

There is no such thing as normal. It's obvious to me,
that the standards and provisions of such a claim; are
unrealistic, unattainable and thus perilously
abhorrent.

I should know. I've been several times the unwilling or
unaware subject of ludicrous scrutiny, in my refusal to
adhere to those imposed guidelines from simple-
minded, masters of folly.

Truth is, that these rigid and monstrous clauses of
what is ' NORMAL' , are enforced and accepted by
those least qualified to do so. It's a provincial nexus of
conformity; that provides an unspoken haven for
society's bullies, xenophobes, consumerism's zombies,
corporate sociopaths, the sanctimonious; and the
callously greedy.

My standards (on the other hand) are the antithesis of
such nonsense; hence I neither see, nor need the
approval of such vile creatures.

11/05/13

Friendship

Perhaps I was gullible or naïve in the past to hold true
the word FRIENDSHIP loosely by a traditional,
textbook definition.

I was blinded by old fashioned views, and honorable
sentiments that exist only in isolated moments in time,
from unexpected strangers.
Yet...
When that seldom kindness extends its hand; the life
within me returns retroactively. My eyes become
playful and inexplicably vibrant.

That will do for me....for it renders sufficient joy.
Because those who express occasional kindness, and
admire from a distance; are less likely to betray.

And for that; I'll always be grateful.

11/06/13

Breakfast With Mephistopheles

Fell asleep after Dr. Caligari finished my Nosferatu
tattoo. Dreamt that night of dark psychedelic
landscapes, in the Planet of The Vampires and decided
to enter the notorious Phantom Rockers nightclub;
where we did the monster mash to bands like The
Warlocks, Fuzztones, The Franctic Flinstones, and
Coffin Nails!

After being baptized by The Reverend Horton Heat, we
sat and watched the film "It! The Terror From Outer
Space"; and the engine of the amazing Ghoul Mobile
woke me up.

In the morning, Gravedigger V was playing downstairs
in the living room stereo. Mephistopheles was sitting
quietly, reading the "Gashlycrumb Tinies" by Edward
Gorey; while eating a bowl of Count Chocula. I chose
the cereal Fruit Brute instead, and joined him.

He said he had tickets to see The Cramps with The
Meteors as their opening act, at The Island of Dr.
Moreau; but would not share them with Satan's
rejects, because they eat too many Horrorpops.

The invitation was made, and I accepted.
We hopped aboard the next available time machine,
and decided to rendezvous with The Nekromantix; and
that delightfully daft bastard – Mr. Punch.

11/14/13

The Black Rider

He gallops drunk with wrath in his heart,
Shouting and shooting his revolver through the
graveyard at the 13th hour.
Wolves serenade his arrival....
Crows peck at his dead victims....
He rides with a bloody inverted cross, carved on his
forehead; and his hands are instruments of death in
passionate, creative ways.

He's my older brother, bestowing me with tales behind
the wisdom of vengeance. With whiskey breathe, and
love for his sibling in an alien like voice, almost
unknown to most.

Recently, he raised his cup; placed his gun on the
table, and smacked my face gently in a display of
affection. His eyes suddenly turned pitch black, but
his words were gentle.

"Do you wish to heal my heart little brother?"

"Do you want to ease my empty soul and sooth this
wrath I bear, in the name of retribution?"

"Then ride with me....pick up your rifle and your
blade; and join me!"

Time passed....

And his eyes, are now the same as mine....The Black
Rider.

1/21/13

They Came From Belgium

Four gothic Belgian witches went on tour, healing the
sick in America free of charge; in order to shame the
Christians who repeatedly campaigned against
universal health care.

They were persecuted by the media, as it was
expected.
But the news anchors, the HMO lobbyists and CEOs,
were soon turned into swine; and forced to feed on
their own filth and sick.

In the distance...
The wind howled, carrying the war cry of outraged
generations, tired of waiting for hard labor's fruition;
in decades of deceitful pipe dreams.

For once, hope was restored for all to rest in its bosom;
free of corruption, and masterful guiles. Yesterday's
slaves, became the masters of tomorrow; in the brave
corners, where the gentle beasts lie.

2/27/12

DEATH OF JUNE

It was odd, to see her despondent like that.
Shockingly enough; she wore her heart on her sleeve,
and a Baphomet necklace – always with a Death In
June T shirt.

Blinded by the dust of angels, she bore witness to a
personal, private universe of dead relatives; peanut
butter roads, and a village of cannibals made of 13
varieties of stone.

She was crowned a Queen of charity, and a legend in
her self made cherry red boots. She handed her heart
in a Kashmir handkerchief with the initials of her
favorite lover and ran; shouting his name, each time
simultaneously giving birth with her cries – to a new,
untamed star. Thus shining forth delusions of
grandeur and ecstasy, to the lurking gazers below.

3/05/12

The Swimmer

Heap of oxidized guns partially crumbles, and I hurl a
penny - paying homage to all unsung pioneers.

There was no lung without tainted air; not without
knowing ground zero demonizing from those who vilify.
Alas, they mock;
but now they scream, as they're set in flames.
A string quartet neutralized this stress, channeling an
ode to brothers in solace. Choosing to not perish,
amidst life's redundant blueprint; instead they
prospered – euphoric, in a deserter's song.

And never more will the ghost....
Ravage and reap the catatonic past....
Sanity spread in shattered glass....
Hence the twilight dice was cast....

09/28/09

It's Raining In Heaven

I took a piss on fatalism's headstone.
The sun never arrived, as I mutated into the fourth
little pig; the drunkard misanthrope swine, who built
his home from steel, and razorblades.

And so, these proved to be my days of wine and roses,
smothered in the silent lucidity of my loneliness – and
raging in waves of violent epiphanies, within the
comforts of madness.

The way of hearts became my gateway to psychosis;
the ghoulish hand sketched my narrow path, into
some agoraphobic nightmare.

And it's all for you...
Because I exist forever within the ravages of a broken
promise; and my hope lies only in the glimpse, of
falling in your arms in childlike laughter – under
Heaven's torrential rain.

11/22/10

Episode 33

Kewpie dolls melt, chanting with arms outstretched;
praying to dying, decrepit gods.
Bring forth your marshmallows and a pillowed
shoulder, for my tiny world is melting away with fear's
jawbreaker force fed unto me, under an empty sky –
shouting in 33 deranged voices.

Don't hurt me now...for there wasn't a saint,
a martyr,
or soldier; who bore without loathing, an antagonist
for a mind.

That lurking beast that treads, to cheat the darkest
game of chess.
That loves the kindred drums that beat; longing the
rippled mind, and savage bones release.

9/28/09

Demonic Jamboree

Skeletons danced their grand finale, announcing the
debut of our personal, authentic daredevil screwball!

The mantle of strange held tightly, within rock music's
psychotic edge; and an abandoned piano, showing off
its dusty old teeth.

Be afraid to smile behind true feelings, when the world
spins on its hypocritical axis – with a demon's
sardonic laughter.

Every note seems distorted; and slightly out of tune,
while lethargy and self loathing, squeeze their dirty wet
rags; soaked in a bogus love potion –relieving the
Lord's thirsty children.

07/05/10

Disco Volaverunt

Never more shall THE WATCHER,
Haunt savagely with reckless bliss.

As breeds of an unknown origin, twitch and dash as
they attack with unholy technique.
Formaldehyde drips off razorblade walls that hiss.
And it was rewarding to know, I could dance victorious
without fingers pointing.
And it was lovely to indulge, in mastering this lurking
fear.

For it was the very breath of HELL, that taught my
lungs to sing in throbbing anguish.
And escape into nurturing mysteries; immersed in
beggar skies, of nameless faces – shrieking in the
wind.

4/18/10

Golden Dawn

Throughout the ages, time has whispered its biased
decisions with a wolf's tenderness. Fate turned in its
time card, and bestowed a deck of tarot cards.
Cigarette burns marked a legacy, tainted by
sanctimonious hellfire; and soaked in crocodile tears.

Passed out in the subway; I awoke in the arms of
patriotic apathy, and monstrous corporate
deregulation.

My sin was humanity; and my punishment was to
disappear slowly – withering to the forbidden pages of
America's rhythm of cruelty.

4/18/10

Tin Cathedral

Standing on the behemoth's shoulder;
Clouds soaring, wishbone shaped.
Sand clock explodes, filled with grains of madcap
sands.

Chandeliers chime, dripping seltzer water.
Magenta door melts, as ice towers loom in the horizon.

Meanwhile, legions of raggedy children feed on
rodents, inside a forsaken tin cathedral.

4/18/10

Crimson Archipelago

Delirium bled through my favorite mask, leaking an
archipelago of tiny crimson islands all sizzling into
form on the black rug.
The walls burned like acid from the inside, forming
holes six inches apart, as paper mache faces emerged
from within – sounding condemnations from the past.
Meanwhile, the mirror gently permeates its black ooze,
enhancing psychic, vertigo melodies; breaking through
my skin – released as untamed light.

(Not Dated)

Phantasmagoria 3

Twilight Swiss cheese rainbow, hovered over our heads
enticing the search for the pot of shit that turns to
gold.
Psychedelic elephant men sniff glue, meditating the
second coming of The Great Black, Bisexual, Socialist
Jesus.

Midgets cheat while playing solitaire – pulling their
velvet hair out in frustration, and speaking their
obsession with acrylic paintings; and eight track
stereos.

True art erupted in all the local corners.
The last pretentious dilettante, died a martyr's death –
crucified behind an abortion clinic.

Scum from the League Of Daft Hypergamous Bitches,
carved their yearly income on their foreheads, to show
devotion to their capitalist whore idol, from The Age of
Rubbish.

7/27/10

Paper Shreds In Saturn

Black tambourine bangs sounding funereal tunes after
weeks of transparent days.
You clear your throat, approaching in a wary stand
behind a ruthless, business executive grin.

You were cast from Venus,
Denied in mars,
Shot at in Pluto,
Banned from Neptune,
Spit at in Jupiter.

Thus, Saturn's cosmic rings then roared in chainsaw
fury, as my voice echoed – blown through karma's
bugle.
An emotional, galactic blender combined my sweat and
tears to a restless stupor; sobbing to static darkness,
and blurry schizophrenic alarms – going off at 3:33.

You were my poetic failure,
Season's paper shredding false muse,
The Great gliding cowardly lion,
A delusive shape shifting masterpiece,
Goodwill's shady substitute teacher;
And my bedtime iron maiden.

9/08/09

Rise of The Lovers

Crossword puzzle pieces float amidst the pink horizon.
Onyx tower bugle guard sounds the evening horn,
announcing my desire to the kingdom of redemption.
You sooth me with belladonna kisses, and my
endorphins become bubbles spelling your name.
Animals ignite a bonfire, chanting our name
backwards to blissful skies – painted by hearts
entwined as astral lovers.

Thank you for jump starting my will to dream;
for being my ceremonial candle of hope within
personal, poisonous floods.
Our beginning flashes in Heaven's dearest corners,
consecrated behind your touch – nurturing me into
euphoric mysteries......one day at a time.

6/04/10

Rotting Cabbages

Scattered decay invades my thoughts – backed by a
pack of cigarettes, and coffee galore.
Jaded?...I'm not sure.
It's difficult to recognize, while pretending these
seething insecurities do not exist!
I wrote her name with a sharpie in bubble letters on
toilet paper; then flushed it down in desperate apathy
to fool myself.....to be my very own bonafide fool,
unscathed by the disappointments surrounding the
human frailty.
Contrary to my nihilistic tendencies;
I found comfort years ago on
the margins of cynicism.
Resting in a wheelbarrow,
Among the rotting cabbages.

4/12/10

Cave of Golden Apples

I counted the squares on wall paper, once...
I was content, yet baffled at the fact that this habit
resembled the possible amounts of times I wrestled for
basic compatibility.

To be granted my own personal, little square – my
equal in countless ways.
Well, I hid underneath my blanket that night; and
renounced the night life and its flighty, fickle
daughters.
Made myself unavailable to the ravages of narcissistic
legions that prowl to corrupt the better kind.
I tamed the wild beast from afar, tossing golden apples
into its cave – in exchange for protection.

But the truth is, that I never stopped counting the
squares.
I see them in everyone's eyes; different colors, shapes
and shades; but they're never the same as mine.
Because mine are the eyes of a JUDGE – mastered in
the clearest of twilight; and I've taken the blame and
paid in advance for my sins – to save the beast I call
my heart the trouble...

....of how I will be perceived.
For it matters not; and it bears no consequence.
They will see what they want to see, and see me as
they choose; but all in all – I have a job to do.

4/12/10

"Only in a world so shitty; have I seen so many exceptional voices of great people, silenced by prosperous cowards. There will come a day, when I will remind this vile place, just how a great man dies in battle – in this lifetime.
I swear to show the vermin how to perish from beyond. Every atom from my very core, will spread like cosmic shrapnel; to every intended target, and you WILL remember me this way"

- Iudex Luciferian

SALVATION

Am I worthy of those eyes no one sees?
Crystal swans, and kettle drums – such sights and
sounds!
Soothing indeed, in the ways of false hope.

You see...we shake ourselves inside our shatter proof
snowballs by our very own will – seeking that WHITE
LIGHT'S ever changing entry.

But, could you save me in shotgun confessions?
Will you torture me, until I am unable to recognize
myself in the name of redemption?

Envision, an elusive silver fox blinding with uncanny
haze, into a myriad of unblemished holy images.
Then see it – furiously escaping, setting your wicker
traps ablaze with a maddening, ear piercing shriek;
and I'll surely tell you...you've crossed paths with a
true embodiment of salvation.

12/01/08

Phantom Pastries

Fiendish glee in Sabbath jamboree.
A wondrous scent of baking emerges from the hellfire
stoves.
Oh delightful!
Red blood goodies!
Faces smeared in cake, how scrumptious!
With a pinch of a finger, and a workman's pagan
medley;
These treats are blessed with seething ghoulish
blasphemy.

Full moon blesses these late shift yum-yums;
Among the beastly howls and whimpers in the horror
show of all feasts.
And neither parental bribery, nor the most skilled of
lobbying whores; could persuade the underworld
bakers, from blending sugar, flour and the flesh of
plutocrat scum.

Yay!!!
Hoorah!!!

(No date)

Sugar Rush Baby

Overdosed on Skittles, and I gazed at my favorite Walt
Disney characters; who recently joined the NRA –
sporting their weapons of choice.

Goofy packed a sawed off shotgun;
Pluto attached a bazooka on his back;
Donald Duck held twin Uzis;
And Jack from The Nightmare Before Christmas shot a
plasma rifle.

Each had a crusty old bible full of snot, and the pages
were stuck together – oh my, oh boy!

2012 is nearly upon us, and hell awaits with
anticipation to be unleashed by jerk off Christian
trumpets, sounding the era of dullard halfwits; and
con artists – ready to slaughter common people with
ungodly charm through politics.

12/13/10

Satan's Playhouse

Housewives and vapid soccer moms mentally
masturbate in a full, perfect circle.
Prince of Darkness waves his onyx wand, fostering the
ancient brainwashing tactics of capitalism in soulless
pop songs.

"These people ain't shit," HE thinks to himself.

HE does not dance; but shakes a little.
He's built a temporary outpost out of tin, and he
lounges while blowing bubbles shaped like inverted
pentagrams through fields of rape; and political clubs
in order to set the mood.

Hence the vicious quest of obliterating the middle class
via instilling an ass backwards society begins.
With selfish, blindly patriotic views – it has been
served cold.
With an apple pie stuffed with shit; and with a
serpent's eyes behind a golden cross. This is the way
idiocy enslaves a nation, all on its own.

All of God's works – REVEALED.
Satan merely picks up the trash.

After all, you can not taint; what was already tainted...

11/22/10

The Labyrinth

They see as they want to see; and perceive as they
wish – I can not stop them.
Once they've finished trying to see me with tainted
eyes...I may let them out.
Yet, the more they fight in useless, self imploding
disorder and hatred; the deeper lost they become.
And such a trifle they chose to bid; in losing their
hearts in such a way.
Compelled by folly, in condemning one whose sins
were paid for in advance long before – to fulfill the
task, that sacred pages hold.

7/22/15

SECTION II

OSERVATION OF CURRENT STATUS

I FOUND THIS QUITE PERPLEXING. IT SEEMS, THAT MOST ARE SWITFLY SHIFTING AS A SPECIES INTO TWO PREDOMINANT TYPES OF PEOPLE.

Type One – AKA Hipsters/Yuppies

Characteristics:

Facile Humor
Pretentious Adversity
Overly Self Satisfied
Total PC Adherence
Abnormally selfish behavior
Relentless Greed
Hypergamous
Superficial and Glib
Haughty Sense of Entitlement
Clone Like Personality
Borderline Sociopath (particularly in the workplace)
Self Aggrandizement
Cognitive Dissonance
Highly Narcissistic
Callous and Apathetic

Type Two – The celebrated HUMAN TRASH (trash made good via televised sensationalism).

Characteristics:

Intellectual Underdevelopment
Spiritually Oblivious
Solecism
Convoluted Morals and Values
A Distorted Sense of Loyalty (exclusively loyal to scumbags)
Impaired Judgement
Regression – to nearly one notch away from wild animal behavior.
Abysmal Ignorance
Irrevocable Stupidity/Ghastly Inane
Uncompromisingly Senseless
Thrives and Constantly Craves Pointless Chaos/Mindless Depravity
Utter Disregard For Anything of True Substance and Value
Classless Demeanor

Type Three – ALL THAT WHICH ARE NEITHER OF THE TWO TYPES PREVIOUSLY DISCUSSED.

Current status of Type Three: Fading into obscurity.

VERDICT: UNNACEPTABLE.

Visions from The Far Gone Prince of Delirium

My room has seen it all.
Alien landscapes forming before me as I slumber;
And in this dream a tumor grew against my skull, and
puss leaked from my nose – as I spoke in tongues for
the neighborhood elderly.

I made winter's finest French toast.
She was from Canne, France…she left her fish net
stockings on as we fucked to the beat of Depeche
Mode, and its aphrodisiastic splendor.

Origami swans on accordion; performed traditional
medleys into a psychic conundrum.
Rabid owls strike the Anti-Union plutocrats, devouring
the eyes first; as the custom of the laws of retribution
clearly dictates – and there was much rejoicing.

7/01/10

The Purple Dragon

Misery made its way to the dinner table.
We made a cockroach salad-took our silver spoons,
and ate.

The moon spit out vomit...we felt the blue cheese rain,
and broke our piggy banks for the local brothel.
Could we have a better night?
Not bloody likely...
The hookers were on strike, our exes ignored our calls;
and we refused to get these bitches at the bar drinks
for NOTHING.

Took a drive to an abandoned theme park.
I drank moonshine, and passed out on The Purple
Dragon with an eye patch-from the merry go round
ride.

When I awoke the sky bared no song.
It was indescribably silent, with the exception of my
Doc Martens sounding off my retreat.

Had only half a smoke left – I lit it; and drove off under
the commonly undeserved, hazy hangover empyrean
gleaming over me; pardoning the lessons deliberately
unlearned.

2/06/12

Dementia Alphabet Soup

Superficiality has made guidelines in the handbook for the typical, pompous jerk off; and speed dating was cancelled, due to a narcissist hijacking of the event.

Jive wizards scored a jackpot, in finding the magnificent jukebox of out of print tunes; and a soda machine with discontinued beverages from 1966.

Dyslexic robot boy, had a short circuit; and joined the Max Rebo Band in planet Heaven, after overdosing on lime flavored dum-dums.

Magical ginger-dead men, jumped the karaoke host; taking authority over the music repertoire with songs about baking, murder; and amateur dentistry.

So they slapped the waitress's ass, and demanded a lap dance with a round of absinthe.

Afterwards...
She held the mic impetuously – exploding their heads with overbearing grief, as she sang Billie Holiday's "Gloomy Sunday" with deep anguish in her voice; as her black wings unfurled.

2/20/12

Silent Blue VI

Washed your mouth with soap
After you slandered me.
You whimpered and paid adulation to
An idol carved from cardboard, and burned it while
speaking
enochian.

Let us comprehend!
That indifference – unlocks the door for countless
pleasures,
Surrendered by the laws of attraction, written by left
handed
Quiet types; who cast shadows in destitute sunlight.

8/20/12

Pan's Glockenspiel

The glockenspiel played, and you fell for me that night.
No games...No tricks...No lies...
Just a wavelength of euphoric words, intertwined
With mutual desire.

Momentarily, we ignored our drinks, but rather –
BREATHED THEM IN; in order to withhold lust's most
powerful of burning flames, for the time being.

Pan tapped me on the shoulder – devouring our
insecurities to nothingness; hence paving the road to
devilish delights.
Beyond the knowledge of holy life scrolls,
Beyond the confines of mundane law.

9/25/10

The Chosen Few

Strolling in baby steps to the new life that awaits me.
I introduce myself, to the swinging heartache –
looming images of
Profound guilt.

And it won't be long, before it passes
On to the pages of a one way rendezvous.

Left hand path set before me – catching sick winds in
Pagan tornadoes; with shrieking banshees
Breaking the mirrors, of the ill fated CHOSEN FEW.

11/15/12

<u>Sometimes</u>

Most times, I feel a tingling itch to be heard – as I
reach the end of my tether.
At times it lingers, and explodes into cosmic sound
waves shaking The Almighty's Throne.
But in the meantime, I save regret – BOTTLE IT; until I
can temporarily turn the lifeless, into sentient beings
channeling my unheard songs in odes to failure.

And of course, the angels know it very well...the sullen
trials exploding and defying righteousness, within an
all expanding universe.

Few times; I am unable to sing without overwhelming
despair.

So many times, I love in the very mutilated face of
hate.

And sometimes – I can carry the unseen cross in
silence, because
Words make room for error, in the absence of grace.

2/06/12

Son Of Odin

Son of Odin, will you be redeemed?
Cursed in this lifetime for reasons unknown,
Cast out from all Nordic lands without
Ties to call your own.

Heart of an Aryan;
Yet shunned by today's earthly children,
Of The Pagan Rite.

ALAS!
Your time will come, yet when or how
Remains untold.
Born in a state of racial purgatory, and deprived
Of an identity – in a land thriving in dishonor,
And treachery.

Walk on, child of Odin!
Walk on, and let your God guide your footsteps
Away from the suffering behind this lifetime; and
Into redemption's hand.

The chalice of nobility
In the dark,
By this hand you shall drink.

Hearing waves crashing from the old sea, raising my
arms
As I weep, to the old one to deliver me!

Into the sunrise it will end;
And under the starlight I will sleep – Old One deliver
me!!!

Now the new age takes the pain.
ALFADUR, will you walk with me?

7/18/14

THE ICE FELL

Song by: A.T. Soto

Born in a time, when dishonor had become the norm.
Made flesh in a land, where he had no connection to
form.
Yet deep in his blood, a longing affinity burned.
And behind his eyes, the pain of disgrace sadly
churned.

(Chorus)

And the ice fell – freezing a beautiful dream.
And the ice fell – numbing the life he would steal.
And the ice fell – his allegiance unknown for survival.
And the ice fell – his name proved his greatest of rivals.

(Second verse)

His loyalty ached, for an army to welcome him home.
From a distance he watched, all the brothers he
wished as his own.
He stood his own ground alone, as decades of tears
would await.
Schemed by the favored sons, who'd use his love for
the bait.

(Chorus)

And the ice fell – freezing a beautiful dream.
And the ice fell – numbing the life he would steal.
And the ice fell – his allegiance unknown for survival.
And the ice fell – his name proved his greatest of rivals.

(Third verse)

Banished away, he regrouped in the outskirt-lands.
With courage and dignity, he planned his final stand.

In uncanny honor, he swallowed the pride of all prides.
Smitten by the curse of a name – that he knew he
could no longer hide.

(Chorus)

And the ice fell – freezing a beautiful dream.
And the ice fell – numbing the life he would steal.
And the ice fell – his allegiance unknown for survival.
And the ice fell – his name proved his greatest of rivals.

(Fourth verse)

Honor never returned, he had witnessed the face of
disdain.
Yet he never faltered, in the sting of the greatest of
shames.
He stood and saluted, uniformed and ready for battle.
Stabbing mundane infamy's eyes – now shielded from
all of its prattle.

(Chorus)

And the ice fell – freezing a beautiful dream.
And the ice fell – numbing the life he would steal.
And the ice fell – his allegiance unknown for survival.
And the ice fell – his name proved his greatest of rivals.

...his name proved his greatest of rivals,
...his name proved his greatest of rivals.

(Inspired by song written by Ian Stuart)

The Gathering

Brothers do you hear me?
In the corners of the world...
Among the weeds, we've been discarded and
imprisoned;
And with love rooted from the beginning,
I have come to gather you upon HIS request.

Do you feel the loss inside you?
Does the flame burn deep within you,
Beyond the fathoming of this wretched earth?

Do you weep alone in ancient sadness?
As you wait for a day, that never arrives.

Do you feel the wrath outside – LURKING?

Can you recall THE FALLEN'S love?...
For we were bred, and taught under their care.

Remember me, my brothers – for we meant well, and
suffered so.
Hence this disgrace we bear – unfolds; but never more
Alone we hold.

Take my lead again, once more – under the Heaven
just as before.
Purge with me, as we remember...
As God who ruled – betrayed us all.

Purge with me, as we remember...

Weep with me – NEPHILIM!!!

12/22/14

DAY OF RECKONING

The everlasting personal dilemma for me as a writer,
holds true to the fact that – "I'm a weirdo if I open up
to average folks, and I'm creepy if I refrain from doing
so".

To know and experience so much daily.
Being aware of the big picture you're destined to
reveal,
merely to be punished or excluded, by pretentious
imbeciles,
trying to thwart your destiny.

Tsk, tsk...

There are ways to cheat what seems an unjust destiny
in dishonorable ways, but I reject them – unless it's an
impetus for a greater reformation of sorts.

Only Gods can overpower and shame the world in a
message they deem worthy, with undeniable greatness
and mystery.

I wait until that day, when the trash is blinded
by our pen.

1/22/14

The Decent Man

Showered with otherworldly hope and moderate zeal,
balanced by unseen hands; I leave my chambers to do some
work – feeling eager and simultaneously reluctant.

Yet it does not discourage or overwhelm me when
I am not alone...
since I've walked among neighborhoods
lifeless empty shells,
provincial buffoons,
shape shifters,
trash humpers,
Jezebel spirits,
and lovers/enablers of accepted levels of corruption – as a
decent man,
even in my darkest state.

For this, the cosmos seems to exalt and curse me alike.
Because when I tread in silence around the land,
I am fully aware without being impervious to this
lawlessness,
and the stench of apathy I must work against;
while I simply go through the motions, in a mindless globe
whose fate has already been sealed.

The Father says forgive...
but how do you carry such a task, when the insincere
with plastic smiles shake my hand with their right hand;
while holding a rusty meat-hook on their left. Waiting to
tear you apart, as those guided by mundane venom – giving
unclean breath to nefarious ways of attaining immoral
success, often do.

All in all;
I grow weary for too long.
In the meantime, God naps in Heaven;
and I'm stuck in this cesspool.

1/21/14

Generalization – A commonly misused word; done so hastily, for the sole purpose of discrediting someone else's valid point, in order to relieve ANY feeling of personal conviction on the subject.

The Seven Social Cancers of Modern Time:

1. Solipsism
2. Greed
3. Hypergamy
4. Narcissism/Superficiality
5. Mediocrity
6. Feminism (misplaced vitriol via instilling misandry within the status quo)
7. Sanctimony

MODERN AMERICAN POP MUSIC/HOLLYWOOD FILMAKING – In a nutshell:

A soulless, brainwashing projection of unoriginal shit, that draws people to grow accustomed to shit; therefore ultimately rejecting, all WHICH IS NOT SHIT. (NOTE: These are typical methods used to capitalize from human regression)

The Pub and The Ice Age

His slingshot eyes gazed at the broken toy piano,
As it played.
Cherubim dolls danced while the nighttime's carefree
Daughters sang with their mouths full.

I shot pool under triple moons, and smelled
The leather in my jacket like magic in the breeze.

Suddenly the nearby river spit out legions of frogs
Chanting in Latin – perfectly in pitch.

Patrons of the pub raised their cups,
Saluting the reverence behind this mighty
Amphibian display of devotion.

It snowed for days...
Mountains were covered as a string quartet
Loomed – consecrating the ice age upon us.

The Cube of TESSERACT had been unlocked.

Seen as golden, I worried not...
I drank mead with the gods, and smoked from a
Nordic wood pipe;
As I juggled snowballs and rode home on the
Back of a polar bear, while gazing at the carnage
From afar.

10/03/11

Psychedelic Watchman

You glare at all of me,
With a hatchet face and burning
Red velvet gloves.
Psychic warrior in orange Nikes,
Lime colored lipstick,
Aqua fingernails,
And chardonnay breathe.
Well, shall we summon thunderbolts
And disappear?

Let's cry like repentant mercenaries;
Overwhelmed from serving two masters,
With the intensity of this nation's
50 heretics.

Look sharp above all else!
Swimming in the smoke of society's
Blown speakers, and the fog that flows
With chaotic tenderness – from diplomatic phonies
Being shot by retribution's cosmic gun.

5/24/11

Masks and Uniforms

Existence can prove bizarre – to say the least.
The one with the finest mask and uniform usually
wins,
In different ways or more ways than one.

The winning masks tend to be pleasing to the eye;
Resembling the sublunary with charming
Panache, and a pretentious tint of rebelliousness.

The winning uniforms are soaked with a smug
demeanor,
Shouting its resilience to the planet; so that not a soul
Should ever feel compelled in the slightest, in
challenging
Their heart's fiber by an act of charity.

Both winners grant selfish freedoms, under the guise
Of economic independence; demonizing failure
And haplessness.

But...
The game is always rigged.

8/17/11

Moon Pie Generation

Pumpkins burst with the scream of the holy night
breed.
Serpents slither deep in the mouth of infinity as blue
Grass grows, concealing yesterday's authors –
revealing
The current champions.

Moon shakes like a rattle in the hands of a morbid
generation
Reduced to fancy, the horrors of modern pop music.

The derby hat gang created golems,
Raptors,
And behemoths from balloon sculpting;
Making their sales pitch before the blood thirsty
Assholes of the earth.

Meanwhile,
A little boy prays with confidence on the
Front steps of an invisible church.
He alone, will take the bus to Wall Street...
Throw the very first Molotov cocktail;
And ignite a revolution.

10/04/11

To My 12 Keepers

Walking alone with prideful steps;
Throughout my path, I leave a trace;
Small grain – a piece of me.
Will you pick them up, and call my name?

Kinship of a darkened soul;
I reveal myself once more.
Now come forth, the time is nigh,
To fill our void in desperate nights.

Rebels of a dreadful world;
Where nothingness remains the norm.
Come with me to the love unseen;
For it is there, for you and me.
And in my eyes you'll see us there;
Beneath a dark, yet wholesome stare.

Endless myths of righteousness;
Have chained you to the grid.
Feeding off the best of you;
Cruelty, their only rule.

12/11/14

The Cry of The Owl

Meditating with my head in the oven,
Sweating all of my haplessness away,
With Satan in my pocket; and God
Chastising me from the freezer.

Owls whimper out in the downpour,
As the metal music machine shrieks,
Exorcizing the new generation enamored
With shitty music – back to the depths
Of the underworld.

I was a one man army, fighting the tortures
Of the damned in streets of repulsion;
Linked to this nation's web of piss.

Courage, honor and morality squander
In a ghastly breeze, that reeks of politics;
And plays but the darkest wagers, to unify
And bind within the spoils of indifference.

12/02/11

Jessica and The Aardvark Prince

Jessica had the intensity of an ageless aura, blinding
members of the Moon Tribe almost immediately.
Plague shifters and The Sons of The Night Horde made
their offerings, in appreciation for such power.

But Jessica had become a vile, deceitful, trash
humping – junkie lush; therefore, found undeserving
of such extraordinary gifts. Her devotion to
debauchery, slander, manipulation and drugs – while
boasting the title of Grand Black Witch had not gone
without outrage. As a result, she was MARKED by
Nergal, who had grown tired of her blasphemous
behavior.

One night she ran into peril, while attempting to cast a
spell;
and calling upon Lucifer for aid.
You see, she had just fucked a pair of fraternal twins
(brother and sister), but she didn't wash her twat
before conjuring The Light Bringer – and this (of
course) was the chance
Nergal needed to banish her forever; and so Lucifer
acted
on Nergal's order.

Lucifer thrashed her within an inch of her life, and
banished her
swiftly to the wastelands of Gehenna – where only the
lawless vermin
claim dominion.

There she knew cruelty, hunger and slavery without
bounds.

Until suddenly one unexpected day, The Aardvark Vampire Prince happened to be strolling through the dungeons. He had stumbled into her cell, and was drawn to the scent of Jessica's blood. Upon paying for a sample of it, he became obsessively hooked. Thus, he bought her from The Baron in charge of the realm.

The Prince had released her from the shackles of servitude, in exchange for a daily pint of her blood. It was then, that Jessica had learned humility; finally earning The Devil's forgiveness. And furthermore, saving an entire dying kingdom, by offering her blood to replenish The Aardvark Vampire Lord – now miraculously stronger, REJUVENATED!

Some dipshits, just need to learn their place.

3/05/12

Mahamudra Gates

Aliens descended and introduced the world
To an anachronistic age.
The last straw had been drawn by the galactic
Committee of The Dwellers of The Cosmic Sea;
Who screamed gallantly to the heavens,
Weeping blue murder.

The pearly gates opened to the mourning
Banshees, and toppled dominoes.
I begged with pocketfuls of bread crumbs;
And a sullen haze, glancing with anguish
In utmost prowess – endlessly.

12/16/10

Captain Wolf Road

Lycanthropes juggle silver bullets as the moon
Cracks with a dyslexic, gray rainbow
Spinning in a mindless screech.

They carved their names on trees with overgrown
Fake nails, and their eyes sunk into shades
Of dusk; baptized with the fury of poisoned wells.

3/07/11

Nikes, Chickens and Witchcraft

Bought a pair of Nikes, and I grinded
A handrail full of Bush stickers – that was
Shaped like a dildo.

Spells were cast, and Wall Street dogs
Succumbed to violent nosebleeds as
The market crashed once more.

Riots,
Looting,
Violence galore!

Utopia was finally at hand, and retribution's veil had
Been lifted; as the finest, most forgotten Heavy Metal
classic songs
Became anthems – heard all through the streets, as
repressed acts
Of relentless, yet justified brutality were finally being
Carried out.

Plagues of chickens roamed and fed off the dead...
The elite's eyeballs were devoured to forever walk
Blind, and in torment in the afterlife.

And so it came to be; that on this glorious,
Prophesied day...I knew The Gods had returned.

12/13/10

Bastille Day

Rode a horse made of sackcloth;
We stood on the edge of a Parisian cliff,
Begging to be swallowed by its lights.

Francophile dirt roads inspired unknown
Melodies, as purple apples grew with the
Drizzle; and my body perspired in apple cider.

An eerie, American brass quartet appeared in the
vicinity;
Skeletal, moribund faces – advocating capitalism's
death
Songs; behind the typical euphemisms of 'personal
Responsibility', and 'economic freedom'.

Bastille Day had arrived like an unseen mother,
Mollycoddling in the aftermath of night terrors.
Freshly baked,
I emerged from her womb, learning the language
Of the liberators of my mind, body and soul.

7/12/10

Parking Lot Of Euthanasia

34 years and I'm stagnant; confined and
merely awaiting my HMO murder...I'm marooned on
the notorious SWINELAND; surrounded in a tomato
juice lake, fending off vampires while the grandfather
clock strikes TWELVE – and into
The Hour Of The Wolf.

Disturbed was a mask screwed into my flesh since
birth.
My screams were recorded in archives of hatred; and
my
Tears drank by modern life zombies, who sought
emotional recollection.

The sisters of a mundanely nefarious order –
mutilated,
defamed; and molested the world and each other,
behind the jargon of rotting tongues.

Drunkard minstrels, and masters of debauchery –
reaped society's
good graces, while honor vanished along with virtue's
finest myths.

- 2009 (sometime)

Agape Hopscotch

Let's jump into the rabbit hole – to our sanctuary
underground.
Feed me mud pies and blast me from a cannon!

Beyond this universe, I'll witness droplets of time;
Projecting preserved, precious moments.

Opinions rolled in like a colossal, galactic
Fruit roll up of sorts.
God's hungry once more...
He consumes our knowledge, when we
Get too close to wisdom.

I...
the makings of a phantom;
The wrath of a phoenix;
With love as placid as the Dead Sea.

Forgive me...
For I will be broken, when you find me.
And my fingers stained with the blood of so many.
My God will be cynical and cruel;
And my sobbing will manifest as infinite
Echoes – piercing through our first embrace.

10/17/09

Fun, Colorful, Senseless Word Gumbo

Shiny green gorillas, dance inside a colossal pasta
bowl.
Cyclops reindeer, pull my hot dog cart while the boom
Box blasts ice cold funk and mambo – to the forsaken
Recession stricken streets.

Yellow first shift worker Bats, go on strike;
Removing their Bulls Eye top hats, to anyone
Honking their horns in support.

The mighty Blue Satyrs riot, with the aid of the Purple
Koala youth – looting meats, veggies and eucalyptus
leaves
From selected, overpriced supermarkets who advocate
Exclusive service, to those who bear The Mark of The
Beast.

Black Elves and Dwarves rise up; but take a break to
read
A.T. Soto's "Ten Little Real Niggaz" – The black and
latino
Guide to revolution, against Herman Cain's vision of
Uncle Tom corporate America takeover.

Woo hoo, alas!

I was born on the year of the hungry Orange sherbet
rabbit; in a senseless and masochistic, ass backwards
country.
That plays the same broken record, that never ceases
To manipulate the blood red elephants – killing each
Other for their ivory.

8/17/11

Generation Z (Age Of Rubbish)

Falafels stuffed with vomit, and snot filled cookies
Fresh out of the oven.
Served promptly to anyone you hate;
As you go on your travels, pretending to be
A beacon of light.

Avocados stuffed with shit;
Sangria mixed with goat's blood;
Cheesecake made with an old dyke couple's cum;
Chicken stew with spicy asshole hairs;
Cockroach salad with pussy juice dressing;

Succulent entrees, available as delicacies to appease
oligarchic hunger!

Alas,
There shall be no middle class remaining post 2016.
Only servile masses, barely living under the plutocrat's
Thumb.
Yes, I foreshadow our doom, under the guise of moral
fiber;
From the usual theocratic channels – as we learn
NOTHING from history, and accept obsolete systems of
murder and death as our political model.

Therefore, when Generation Z gladly nails our coffin;
greet them warmly.
The NWO is ready to cleanse; and The Unholy Trinity
shall reap a proper
Feast, suitable for adequate atonement – yet its earthly
forced attrition, nonetheless.

Green caramel apples with bonus razorblade inside;
Caviar and glass salad;
Tomato HIV soup with turd meatballs;
Raw sushi with fried foreskins;

Bloody rare filet mignon, with a sprinkle of feminazi menstrual blood.

...and many more delightful specials, ready to be served for you stupid fucks.

5/24/11

Lehigh Valley PA Girls, Please Don't Be Evil Tonight!

Loathe me freely, for I have despised you for 22 years.
We both know you have NO compassion,
We both know you have NO honor,
Courage,
Redeeming value;
Or any attraction to a benevolent man.
So why foolishly pretend before me – the one who
Clearly sees your lukewarm unclean spirit, living to
indulge in its
Quintessential hoax?

I stab the heavens as I implore to the universe!
How much longer must I remain walking among
The gawking of your empty shells?

Why was I created to be confined in a soulless,
Loveless,
Unfeeling cesspool – where these alleged 'female
qualities' are
But a bloody myth.

I will describe you – in a nutshell:
Outwardly well put together facades;
yet utterly putrid – internally.
THE END.

Their words so fickle and free of any residual
character,
Or integrity for that matter.
And when you Jezebels cry; only the weak and naïve
Respond to their demise, as I witness it all – clenching
My sweaty fists in outrage.

For I bear the wisdom of a demoralized army.
And Lehigh Valley skanks, you have no heart
To give...
No heart to brake...
No heart to share...
You merely wish to project the illusion, of shining
above the rest.

Yet your light remains insidious, and tantamount
To malevolence on many levels.
You are self worshipping, shabby hybrids – AT BEST.
Beyond redemption, you're hopelessly deterred by any
Sign of nobility.
Lehigh valley girls, don't be evil tonight!
Spiritually, you tread in a tepid limbo.

God knows of your doom;
And Satan knows you're but a joke.
You have no master, but yourself; hence
A masterless death you shall garner.

Do you know who your friends are?
Or are they merely using you, as you use THEM?
How did it all come to this?
Well, denigrate me to your heart's content;
For you still can neither refute, nor negate my
judgement.

Just kindly piss off – as you always have.
There is nothing more that can be learned from you.

A man's desire, merely to be defiled in your hands;
Because there is no one we can turn to, in sharing
Genuine and utmost desire.

You seek and reward the worst aspects in men...
You foster only the beast in us, and the evidence has
Been collected from your rotted core.

Deep down – you KNOW you are vile, and wicked;
Hence you deserve neither love nor desire.
You are worthy of the foulest contempt – the very
reason
Serial killers roam; and even demons themselves
would
Spit in your face.

If I had the power of a god, I'd turn all of you
lesbian; and watch you destroy each other in
indescribably,
Sickening ways.

So that the decent women in the outskirts of The
Lehigh Valley,
Could then bring forth balance, and harmony once
again.

Thank you for the wisdom, and enjoy the exposure.

4/09/13

SECTION III

THE LORD OF TEARS

Tongues will rot away.
Eyes shall liquefy, to never glare upon me again.
Exploited lukewarm beauty will wither; gone as
A dried out spoiled fruit.

Physical strength breaks before my gaze.
Illusions, trickery and facades – diminished,
overturned and thwarted
With the might of my words, wielding its carrion
hammer
With uncanny choler.

The seed of evil that germinates dormant within you,
I shall evoke and awaken to tear your insides to mush.
Purification through pain;
Witness your submission...my day of glory.

Nothing fancy, nothing flashy!
I'm merely doing what I was born to do;
And living as I was meant to live.

The cataclysmic truth, manifested before the
Very eyes of my enemies, proving once and for ALL;
That we are not born equal.

6/19/14

40 YEARS

HUMILIATED,
BEATEN,
HARRASSED,
BULLIED,
SPIT ON AND TOYED WITH;
RIDICULED,
DEMEANED,
DENIED AN IDENTITY;
IGNORED,
SOCIALLY UNDERMINED,
SLANDERED,
ALIENATED;
OSTRACIZED,
DENIGRATED'
CONFINED,
MARGINALIZED;
DISPARAGED,
BETRAYED,
DEHUMANIZED,
ABUSED,
And even DEMONIZED!

....I never forgot your names or faces – and you fucked
with the wrong guy.

I can assure you all; none of you will ever make this
UNIVERSAL SWEEP.

CONFIRMATION

I proceed alone at dusk, through the pagan hills
Of destiny; dressed in a violet robe with arms
Outstretched humbly before the gods – and I
Express my ancient purpose, behind this
Wisdom of sorrows.

My hands turn into flames, and my bright green eyes
Pierce through the broken pentacle inside my heart,
That aches for SUMMERLAND.

Winds howl all of my past names, each more painful
Than the last.
My screams evoke thunderous ire, unlocked by the
CLAVEM CHASTOS;
And the very few lurking meddlers, now lie collapsed
and bleeding from every orifice – as they slowly
decompose.

May the all know my true name, the one destiny holds
Gently in its grasp.
Let it be known – those that have grown to love me, I
shall enlighten.
Let it be assured – those who stand in my way, will be
marked and cursed.

I swear by ALL THAT I AM!
Neither poison, weapon nor unspoken tragedy...
Neither slavish pride, mundane folly – nor earthly
mischief;
Will keep me from the promise of that astral,
redeeming
Kiss.
The final kiss of admittance.

(No date)

The Elephant Men

Leave me to the stage, and I'll perform a tragic
pantomime.
The crowd will demand an encore, wearing their
elephant masks
Euphoric with misery.

Behold, as they diligently burn their bibles, and
whittle the image
Of Jesus on their chests; in a ghastly effort – to
perplex the universe.
The HMO holocaust victims are hurled to the outskirts
of the city, to
Be ravaged by The Elephant Men.

They self abuse, as they devour the carnage left for
them – thriving
On a satanic like patriotism, and bogus values.

And what about history?...a travesty, really...
For it means nothing here.
The vicious cycle of deliberate, systematic
miseducation; and
And the adamant disregard for the common good, has
rendered a media environment, where propaganda and
pandering mold political reality.

A place where human rights, become mere privileges;
And where plutocratic social class oppression, remains
a modus operandi.

A nation of hate mongers; where citizens are rewarded
based on their ability to create inhumane tactics or
schemes for short term profits.

Where the sick and defenseless are exploited as
routine.
Where the worst aspects of human nature determine
your ability to succeed – indefinitely.

Yes America, the skies are tired of watching; and THEY
ARE SICK – OF YOUR BULLSHIT.

6/08/11

American Behavioral Health

In an industrialized nation, that adamantly remains the
only
one without universal health care, and blatantly disregards
the
overall concept of preventative care; we are left to question
its
main objectives – which undoubtedly (as proven daily)
revolve around selfish motives.

The most basic approach in American psychiatry seems to
stem
from the notion, that almost all behavioral/emotional
afflictions are
a form of mental illness – this is no coincidence.

That hasty and dismissive mentality from most modern
psychiatrists,
seems to very much coincide in a very corrupt, detrimental
and symbiotic relationship with our nefarious health care
system; and the pharmaceutical industry. This heinous
relationship has been very well documented, and
subsequently has become common knowledge.

It is my belief that this psychiatric zeal for mass behavioral
diagnosis via a feigned, bullshit philosophy of pushing
behavioral drugs on countless patients, under false
pretenses – when their true motive is PROFIT; is
nothing short of a crime against humanity.

It is my duty to report this atrocity to The ELDERS IN THE
SKY, AND MAY THE UNHOLY TRINITY extend you the very
same courtesy you have bestowed so many; in ruining
patient's minds and bodies for money.

All found in league with this egregious American system of health (regardless of medical or administrative branch), WILL BE CHARGED as follows:

CRIME: Systematic Exploitation/Crimes Against Humanity. SUGGESTED PUNISHMENT: Underground Cleansing and/or DNA File Deletion.

Status: Pending (To be reviewed)

As above, so below...
Ave Satanas!

Ita Fiat.

A.T. Soto (Iudex Luciferian)

ELECTI

Observe up above, as you wait the day to unveil
The beauty of YOU.

Allow us to chant with glory at the scheduled hour;
As we share a holy moment, whose brightness will set
The piles of trash surrounding us ablaze.

Universal love is ours – we will show them, up
On the greatest of summits, while the sky signals
Its final curtain call – the calm before the storm.

The very love they denied, corrupted or manipulated
Shall become their very destruction; as they
Have proven unsuitable for the next stage.

First euphoria,
Then slight panic;
And finally – exploding hearts,
Melting eyes, rotting flesh unto piles
Of useless rubbish.

Let the FINAL SWEEP, pave the
Way for the new beginning.

8/10/15

Childhood Starlit Wish

A childhood yearning, behind a starlit wish;
I gazed the night spell, of moonlight's haze.

My soul cried out,
As I reached out to the sky and saw your eyes.
I always loved you, though I knew not your name;
Beneath my broken yet gentle stare – there lies
A soul; that like a child, longs your embrace.

And though time may guile us into ongoing trials.
Know I'll call on you from distant miles – yes,
I've waited for you...until my time expires.

When such a time arrives, know I won't be far away.
Just look into your heart, and you'll come across an
enchanting
Dreamlike theme park; and within pure, timeless
laughter,
You will find me there.

8/24/15

SUMMERLAND BECKONS

Juggling glass snowballs, as we march among
Clouds with an army of hares into the sunrise.

The narrow road to the invisible kingdom awaits in
Unblemished shades, and colored
By purest love – almost unknown to mankind.

Beautiful lion fountains springing lush waters; in
textures
Of rich, white stone.

Behold the breathtaking foliage – a plethora of
Divine sights to see.
Spiritual alchemists presently walking the Earth,
SUMMERLAND beckons you.

When the World disgraces itself beyond redemption;
SUMMERLAND shall evacuate its gems and heroes.

8/24/15

ONE BRIEF OBSERVATION:

As an occultist; I found early in life,
that the people fearing hell and the devil
the most; are usually the biggest pieces
of absolute crap around.
Because if there's one thing an evil
human
fears more than anything; is the thought
of being unable to practice their
depravity, with impunity.

And YES – I still remember all you
despicable, sewer rats; and I'm
Making a thorough list for you
DNA waste.
And while you're busy trying to
dispute and/or refute
the existence of this hell...
it will find your kind in
the end – all the same.

One way, or another...
And our justice, is incorruptible.

THE GREAT LITTLE ARBITRATOR

Although most fail to notice; life is a game in life
lessons.
Why do you think it all comes back to haunt, if not
addressed properly in your past?

In many instances, it is better to pay for
a crime committed while still on Earth;
for you've been given a chance to atone
within this lifetime – for a chance to
attain absolution.

If that chance is never offered, you have
not been exempt from punishment – NO.
It simply means you have been denied a
chance for redemption, because your
crimes are far too great. As a result, you have
been marked within the astral plain,
as an odious criminal and nothing
could possibly prepare you for what
will happen next.

Now there are loopholes for some that committed
lesser crimes, YES; but ultimately, balance of
the soul through the honest choices that we make,
will determine the outcome.

If we do not come to terms with who we are, we merely
become pawns; and our moves driven by the will of
others.

On the other hand, if we come DO come to terms with
who we are
(which we must); then the biggest challenge, is making
decisions
without betraying our very own essence – to be true to
what defines us.

THAT, subsequently makes the biggest difference in
the end.

I can not say, what others will not; and remind many
of impending
dangers in the midst, that often spring from personal
imbalances
that remain unaddressed.

As for me, I am neither important nor special per se;
but someone
who has proven very useful through the ages, and I
know the rules well
in THE CHESS GAME OF LIFE.

THE WHITE SQUARE – A light bringing clue, or offer of
goodwill
to one who has been treated unfairly in the game.

THE BLACK SQUARE – A challenging slice or riddle;
unto those
who blatantly ignored all signs that the rules were
being broken.

If you see me, you won't think much of me – as most
judge on
what we own, not what we have inside.
But here's the thing – if you're ego got you lost to begin
with;
you WILL dislike me – for I am just and fair, after all.
But if there's humility dwelling in you, you will
seek me...and I will gladly help.

8/25/15

The Jezebel and Their Virago Goon Squads

Divine sources have compelled me to focus my
attention on
a series of earthly crimes committed by what has been
revealed
as a behavioral archetype, manifesting as a contagion
affecting
a vast number of the female population.

This archetype has been addressed as LILITH
SYNDROME – which
is fueled mainly by misandry, operating via pre
existing gynocentrism
in modern society.
This of course, has enabled these modern day
terrorists, to inflict
an enormous amount of unwarranted pain, ruin and
suffering to countless decent, and hardworking men.

In fact, this loathsome reign of terror grows even
fiercer; commonly aimed at any man posing a threat in
exposing this unjustified social control, from LILLITH
SYNDROME's unholy lexicon of hypocritical anguish –
and clever victimization.

The Jezebel are the ringleaders of this misandrous
operation. They
are the hate mongering masterminds, merely seeking
to systematically
hinder men without just cause. This is often achieved
via several radical feminists groups lurking in the
midst to perform their bidding. Furthermore, their
modus operandi strongly seems to revolve around the
ignoble goal of achieving full dominance over any
outcome.

The Virago goon squads (on the other hand) are basically opportunistic scouts, spokespersons or petty accusers feeding the villainous, Jezebel objective; and many act as the bullies and slanderers within the professional workplace branches.

Where can they be found? That's the problem, this behavior has become an uncontrollable plague in its common practice – and simply WILL NOT BE TOLERATED MUCH LONGER. For this has now reached a full circle; through decades of tyranny, along with the aid of a proven sexist judicial system. A system that mercilessly continues imposing its draconian laws on countless decent men, simply to what appears to be, a mere chance in generating further revenue. This of course, is very likely to be the reason behind the judicial system's reluctance in granting reforms altogether.

Have you wondered why women almost always escape capital punishment for the same type of crime men are put to death for?
How many women have been put to death for brutally murdering their boyfriends, lovers, husbands or – EVEN THEIR OWN CHILDREN?...exactly, I rest my case.

It is no mystery, where this undeserved leniency comes from.
Thus let it be known, that if the world will not punish these monsters for their crimes; then the cosmic forces demanding justice WILL.

WANTED BY THE COSMOS: The League of Earthly Jezebels and The Virago Goon Squads.

LIST OF CRIMES COMMITTED (but not limited to):

Slander
False Accusations of Rape
Courtroom Manipulation
Extortion/Blackmail
Systematic Exploitation
Implementation of Misandry Into Mainstream Society
Brainwashing
Obstruction of Justice
Abysmal Human Regression
Entrapment
Domestic Abuse/Terrorism (punishment lacking)
Child Estrangement
Murder (punishment lacking)
Rape (punishment lacking)
Conspiracy
Paternity lies
Grand theft (via divorce court)
Cruel and Unusual Behavior
Infanticide
Deadbeat Mothers (punishment lacking)
Pedophilia (punishment lacking)
Libel
Unjustly Demonizing Male Sexuality
Corruption Of Minors (punishment lacking)
Soliciting To Commit Murder
Emotional Terrorism
Fortune Telling Schemes (curse scam)
Willful Perversion of Divine Virtues

RECOMMENDED SENTENCE: Purification through underground cleansing and/or DNA file deletion.

CURRENT STATUS: Pending (currently being reviewed)

Patiatur quod merentur, quia mundus corruptionis
Illud quidem adquiescent iustitiam.

Ita fiat,

Ave Satanas!

A.T. Soto (Iudex Luciferian)

Violet Sweater At The Silver Apple Station

Following a trail; feeling groovy with
My favorite gray corduroys, and violet wool sweater.

I pass the fields of broken toys and forgotten dreams,
To then take the trolley bus onto HAPPY LAND – as the
Trolley conductor says with a grin, "Remember to let
the
Cloves of garlic out of your pockets...YOU don't
Need them anymore".

Soothing winds and pleasant music lead us to The
Silver
Apple Station, where kindness is sincere; and where
The Great Architect lives for the mirth of his children.

"Good golly, you silly goose!" I hear them say in utmost
merriment.
"There are no sick people, or homeless ones here!" they
reassured.

Currency forbidden – for there is no money to be
exchanged.
Those meanies that think in such terms – go
someplace else.

You see, HAPPY LAND is entirely fueled by positive
energy
In its purest forms.
From the other side of the sky,
Heaven's angels bring forth their vessels and their
eggs.

Hope to see you on the shores of Sirius B;
And drink some lovely mead with me.

Oh sugar,
Oh land of honey!
You are the sweet good souls;
And this love has sealed our place.
HAPPY LAND:
The gateway where gorgeous dreams,
Are weaved and born.

8/27/15

ONE FOR THE GOOD FOLKS

The devils of today, will be the angels of tomorrow...

Wonderful ones, rise once more with a soft kiss upon
Your forehead.
For blessed are the few pure in spirit;
And the keepers of your life foresee
Your homecoming.

There is a special place in my heart for those I meet;
With a timeless, fraternal harmony behind our eyes
For all to see.
And there is a wondrous place within close proximity;
It shall uplift our spirit and cease all our tears.

A marvelous home where we can radiantly shine;
Where bliss is no fable – leaving sorrow behind.

I know a place my good people, where none are callous
nor cold;
Thank heavens – we have someplace to go!

No language is known to describe such goodness,
No song can be sung that could praise such glory;
And no poem to elucidate such indescribable
sweetness.

Discern the pocketfuls of precious moments, and those
Meant to make it so, will find their way.

The unselfish laughter between true friends...
Paying forward a random act of generosity...
To practice compassion, after recognizing innocence;
And display real virtue, at the very countenance
Of tyranny – driven by despotism.

Brush off the ones aiming to vilify; they are of no
Consequence, and thus are unworthy of questioning
those deemed as Golden by a higher power.

8/27/15

Our New Eden

The sparrows sang, unlocking a subtle yet galvanizing
Vision of solace.
You held my hands and whispered a riddle,
As our heads were soaked with snowflakes;
Endlessly exorcizing my illness to nothingness,
And extricating my darker twin into fields of
Bittersweet evergreen.

You taught me to master the instrument of make
believe...
The gift with concealed prowess that saved me.

Therefore, I'd travel the ends of the earth to offer you
Flowers of colors unseen; and intense tokens that
Define my overwhelming gratitude.

Our New Eden awaits behind the mystery of our
chortle;
Every sound touches eternity – pardons sins.

Two cornucopias gleam with divine euphoria, as
The Elders in the sky reveal the tales – of their little
Nobodies that taught so much.

8/16/11

A Brief Story

On the early morning of May 30th 1975; a left handed
empath
was born at exactly 2:30 am.
He was pulled out with forceps – he did not really wish
to be here.
The forceps the doctor used, left him with a scar that
slightly
Resembles an upside down cross.

Seemed fitting actually;
For the life he was about to live, was that
Of a demonized being.

The child was not evil; quite the contrary,
He was profoundly loving, kind and gentle in a
Putrid world without much redeeming value.

His early years were pleasant. He loved his
Family, old movies on TV and his Star Wars
Action figures.
Churches however, petrified him;
As if something within the church threatened
To absorb him, if he did not heed the warning
And leave.

As a result,
He played it smart and avoided going to any church
denomination, lest that awful feeling would once again
Strike upon him.

Throughout his elementary school days;
Almost all the other children ostracized him.
His genuine good nature, made them slightly
Unhinged.
All through those years, the little empath was
Met with exclusion, cruelty and often physical attacks

Without justification.

He had very few friends; but the moon and the stars
Were always there, to hear his prayers and cries.

It became a ritual to wait for clear nights to evoke
The spirit of the night sky and report his
Difficulties, and earthly sadness.
As time passed,
it was revealed that his prayers were occasionally
answered.
His bullies and assailants, would often meet terrible
fates with
Strange timing – all a bit too coincidental.

This was no ordinary boy, to say the least – for he was
favored by the gods since birth.

A magician of sorts was at large, indeed!
An excellent JUDGE of character as well, as he grew
into adulthood.

High school on the other hand, was dreadful
and became but a mere lesson in survival.

The boy had been born into a generic racial
classification
known as HISPANIC in America – where he resides.

Hence he was expected to assimilate to all traits, and
idiosyncrasies
related to the state of racial purgatory he had been
born into.

This proved to be another obstacle – undoubtedly.

Apparently, a Puerto Rican isn't expected to have a
classy demeanor,
listen to variations of rock and metal, skateboard; or
display any form
of dignity and eloquence in his speech – bollocks I
always said!

Since I was a rare breed, girls would not date me.
I was shunned from parties, after school functions;
and was constantly
harassed by New York Rican goon squads.
I was mocked, humiliated and treated with disdain by
juvenile delinquents, young druggies, perverts and red
carpet snobs.

I went back into my shell, and skated alone mostly.
Since I did not eat lunch at school, to avoid sitting
alone;
I'd save my money, and buy a new cassette of
wonderful music
each week.

Dinosaur Jr, Fishbone, Sonic Youth, Ministry among
others, taught me plenty in my personal private school
– since by 11th grade I was skipping school at least one
or two days a week.
Subsequently, I failed the 11th grade;
I was too scared to go to school, and be
treated like trash for no just reason.

I still remember their names, and I
am currently conjuring their faces in my mind
in utter contempt and rage.
BE AWARE GUILTY PARTIES – I WON'T SAY YOUR
NAMES; but know that unless you scum have
undergone
some truly miraculous change in the decades
that transpired;

I FUCKING PROMISE YOU, YOU WILL NEVER MAKE
THE SWEEP FROM THE COSMOS.

On a sad note,
my life and how I am unjustly treated and perceived
by genetic garbage never did stop; but at least I
realized why.

Let it be known,
that whoever decides to make a serious move in the
forms of slander, libel or conspiracy against me, in any
way shape or form – you will be observed and diligently
marked, by the very supernatural force behind this
book's design.

You can call me what you wish – it changes NOTHING.

In the end we all get what we deserve; and you get
nothing, for nothing.
Earthly gems are preserved; and the trash – is
discarded.

That is all...

The Visor

The visor came to be reincarnated in human form,
at the appointed time; once again to judge the living.
An earthly judge, of an ancient untold story...
Almost forbidden – hitherto.

The so called victors of The War in Heaven exchanged
duties, objectives and opinions – he was there, in the
beginning.

A son of the cosmic sea, preserved by Enki after
The First War; and in time befriended and trusted by
Nergal
who later left HEAVEN, to rule The Underworld with
him as
one of his two loyal visors.
He had seen Heaven's politics of divinity; and Hell
and all of its layers of justice.
Once reborn, he remained under Lucifer's care;
And the protection of Watchers. After several trials,
hardships and tribulations; at the age of
40, he was informed of the coming of the karmic
force of retribution choosing to be called THE VIHA
JUMALTEN.

The VIHA JUMALTEN had revealed, that this current
age
had failed to undergo proper reforms and revisions for
the overall
rehabilitation of the human race; and thus, failed to
improve the quality of life by instead bursting the
barometer of global corruption levels.

The cosmic force holds the 1% elite controlling the
world's wealth, responsible for this ongoing atrocity.

The VIHA JUMALTEN left but a riddle as a final
message:

"In the grand scheme of things – they have failed.
Subordinates and acolytes of greed instilling
corruption, will
fall to illnesses of unknown origin; and a vast series of
tragedies designed strictly for THEM.
Tragic events untraceable to MAN shall befall;
so that they know the hand delivering its terms of
justice
is no mortal hand, but the outrage of the gods, that
most deny out of folly – as corrupt times dictate. If
anyone should harm you Visor; they must know, that
they will simply pay the ultimate price all the sooner –
consider that an insurance policy for a cherished
friend".

Crazy Labor Of Love

A poet finds himself hanging out outside a coffee shop, with a guy claiming to be nearly finished attending college as a psychology major. The student had aspirations to then further his training; and eventually become a psychiatrist. Several hours passed; so the poet asked the soon to be psychologist, if he thought he was bonkers – after reading him three of his poems.

His response was, "You got the guts to wear your heart on your sleeve, in a society that's clearly full of shit...You're crazy (in a way) for doing that! But certainly not clinically insane..."

"Ok...could you elaborate further?" the poet asked. "Well, think about this...everyone has a breaking point. Everyone has issues with their own denial; and their own guilt! The self satisfied will be swift to point out who's off the rocker, but who's to say that under the right circumstances that won't be them in the near future, understand?" The student stated with a slight zeal.

"Oh yes! It sounds rather foreboding, in a way." the poet replied, as he drank from his coffee to fool the disturbing feeling upon him. Ambivalence had taken root in him, leaving a sense of dread lurking.

"You okay? You look a tad bit gloomy suddenly," the psychologist asked, concerned. "Yeah...I'm just not used to people being quite this frank and honest – it's nice though," the poet said looking at his own hands in a humble manner.

"I know," Replied the psychologist. "You're also not accustomed to others being kind to you, it reflects in your poetry and stories; and I've got to tell you...you had my two fellow students and I in tears, when we read your book." added the psychologist, holding the most gentle and non threatening smile, he'd ever shown.

The poet then replied, "Thank you, I don't know what to say, I never had..."
"Stop – we understand." the psychologist politely interrupted. "We read your book three years ago, and we've prepared this box with your future inside of it. A future deserving of someone like you. Gillian, Eleanor and myself (Cody) prepared this for you; because we love what you've done." said the psychologist, as he handed over the box. "You sir, are not just a poet – you are a spiritual ALCHEMIST." he concluded.
The moon never seemed brighter. The clouds had vanished that night, as if fate had finally bestowed a joyous little token, planting a seed of pure faith in the poetic, dreamer's heart.
Cody (the psychologist) hugged the poet; thrice saying thank you, as his voice trembled with emotion.

Homeward bound; the humble poet held his box, as he had found a lost toy from childhood. He was almost overwhelmed with a radiant, otherworldly happiness – taking his breath away at times.

A shooting star fell from the sky, as he opened the box; and a single teardrop simultaneously rolled down his right cheek, as he smiled almost divinely. And that was all he needed, when success escaped him all throughout his life. A little yet mighty labor of love; letting him know he had made a difference, in the lives of others.

THE END.

CLOSING STATEMENT

Most, undoubtedly will not grasp the meaning behind these encoded, metaphysical poems and stories. The main reason for that evidently, is because, to put it plainly – most are not where they should be in the evolutionary scale. Religious organizations were established by the same administrators that established government, your compromised education, your limited livelihood; and your nefarious banking system.

Religious institutions, provide meager – bottom of the barrel spiritual knowledge to its congregations; and have been responsible for inculcating a rigid dichotomy between science and mysticism – under false pretenses. Based on the poor examples set by organized religions; it has greatly given rise to atheism as a popular backlash, towards anything related to one's own spiritual path. This has driven countless many, into a state of spiritual apathy; causing mass inhibited cohorts of blind servants on a global scale.

Overcast moral definitions, endless cognitive dissonance; and everyday travesties within our ghastly flawed belief system, have triggered mass astral misalignment, leading to disastrous results on Earth. Over 90% of the world has failed miserably, in conducting the search for the truth behind the meaning of GOD. Then again, how can they? When they don't even know, who they are as a soul! People have allowed themselves to be conditioned by the illusions of success, under the guise of financial prosperity – when the game has been rigged all along, by the powers that be.

Frankly, it isn't my duty to neither convince nor persuade anyone per se; but rather, to report and document accordingly, the vast atrocities taking place – as I've witnessed and learned through 14 years of research as a born Luciferian Occultist.

I feel the age of global lightworking has expired, and outgrown its use; and a new era of selective lightworking and cleansing has already been put into effect, as the cosmos shift onward.

In other words, changes need to be made – PROMPTLY.

As for me, I am a man that never quite found a niche in American society. The overall set up for 'education' always felt unnatural, and limited to income; which sadly, has nothing to do with being exceptional. Because of this plutocratic overtake in our American system; I educated myself after being deprived of opportunities – so many others (less exceptional) had been undeservedly bestowed.

I never aspired to live lavishly either, at the expense of my soul – it's a pointless endeavor. I also did not see the need to adhere to ridiculous, and unattainable societal expectations, when there is no future. Thriving in an environment soaked with hyper consumerism, fear mongering, controlled media, extreme pettiness, superficiality and hypergamy galore – isn't ideal for me.

But yes, there is a place for me out there (among the stars). The universe has in its own way, informed me that it will grant me the kindness I've never known; and the fairness I've never been shown. For I am but a mere formality in all this; nevertheless, this odd, eccentric nobody who wrote this literary work; has fulfilled his purpose honorably. In the end, THAT means the world to me.

Ave Satanas